Magic Molly

MOLLY MAC

by MARTY KELLEY

PICTURE WINDOW BOOKS
a capstone imprint

For Marianne Klemarczyk (MK) and Jo Gargaly and
all my good friends at DJ Bakie School –Marty

Molly Mac is published by
Picture Window Books
A Capstone Imprint
1710 Roe Crest Drive
North Mankato, MN 56003
www.mycapstone.com

Text © 2019 Marty Kelley
Illustrations © 2019 Marty Kelley

Education Consultant: Julie Lemire
Editor: Shelly Lyons
Designer: Ashlee Suker

Library of Congress Cataloging-in-Publication Data
Names: Kelley, Marty, author, illustrator.
Title: Magic Molly

ISBN 978-1-5158-2384-1 (hardcover)
ISBN 978-1-5158-2388-9 (paperback)
ISBN 978-1-5158-2392-6 (ebook PDF)

Printed in the United States of America.
PA017

☆ Table of Contents ☆

All About Me!

A picture of me!

Name: Molly Mac

People in my family:
Mom
Dad
Drooly baby brother Alex

My best friend: KAYLEY!!!!

I really like: Crunchy delicious tacos! But not if they have tomatoes on them. Yuck! They are squirty and wet.

When I grow up I want to be: An artist. And a famous animal trainer. And a professional taco taster. And a teacher. And a super hero. And a lunch lady. And a pirate!

My special memory: Kayley and I camped in my yard. We made s'mores with cheese. They were surprisingly un-delicious.

Chapter 1

REAL Magic!

Fwwwwwwiiip. Ffffwwwwwwwwip. Fwwwwippppp!

Molly Mac shuffled a deck of cards on her school desk Monday morning. She picked up all the cards that fluttered to the floor. She put them back in the deck and shuffled again.

Fwwwwiiiiiipp!

Kayley bent down and helped Molly pick up the cards that fell on the floor again. "Molly Mac?" she said.

"Don't ask," said Molly.

"I'm asking," said Kayley.

Molly straightened up the large pile of cards in her hands.

"Yesterday my dad took Alex and me to a theater to see a real, live magician named **Amazing Marvin!**" Molly said. "And he was amazing! Because the word 'amazing' is right in his name! He did tricks with cards, and he had a magic rabbit named Presto and a lovely assistant named Raylala. He made Raylala float in the air and then . . . he put her in a box and cut her in half!"

Kayley gasped. **"He cut her in half?"** she asked. "How?"

"It was **REAL** magic!" Molly said. "Her guts didn't even fall out or anything! Then he put her back together. There weren't even any parts left over like there are when my dad puts something back together. It was amazing!"

Kayley pointed to the deck of cards. "Are you doing magic tricks with the cards?"

Molly nodded. "Do you want to see a trick?"

"Yeah!" Kayley said.

Molly shuffled the cards again. Kayley helped her pick up the cards that fell to the floor.

"That's not the actual trick," Molly explained. "But I am definitely getting very good at making the whole deck appear on the floor. Do you think that might count as a magic trick?"

Kayley shook her head. "I don't think so.
Dropping cards doesn't seem very magical. It
mostly seems clumsy."

Mr. Rose walked by on his way to his desk.
Molly jumped out of her seat and grabbed his
sleeve. "Mr. Rose! Mr. Rose! Do you want to see
a magic trick?"

Mr. Rose smiled. "Absolutely."

Molly shuffled the cards. Kayley and Mr. Rose helped her pick up all the cards that fell.

"Maybe you should practice a little more, Molly," Mr. Rose said. "If you get better, you can show the class a trick on Friday for Show-and-Tell."

Mr. Rose walked back to his desk.

"Wow," Kayley said. "You could be a real magician. Just like Amazing Marvin."

Molly nodded. "I'll be even better than that," she said. "I'm going to be Magic Molly. And you can be my lovely assistant, Kaylala. Do you happen to have a giant saw?"

"Do I want to know what you're going to do with a giant saw?" Kayley asked.

"Probably not," Molly answered.

Chapter 2

Disappearing Cookies

Riiiiiinnnng!

The bell rang for recess. Molly and Kayley dashed across the playground to their secret snack spot.

Molly opened up her backpack and pulled out her sketchbook and started writing.

Kayley opened her lunch box and took out her snack. "I have oatmeal raisin cookies!" she told Molly. "My dad made them. They're delicious! I brought some for us to share."

Kayley waved the cookie in front of Molly's face. Molly did not notice.

Kayley ate the cookie. "What are you doing, Molly? It's snack time."

"I'm too busy for snack," Molly said.

"Too busy for snack?" Kayley gasped. "There's **no such** thing!"

Molly tapped her pencil on the page of her book. "I'm working on a list of incredible tricks for our magic act."

She handed the list to Kayley.

Magic tricks for SHOW and TELL

1. Make my lovely assistant float in the air.

2. Make my lovely assistant disappear.

3. Put my lovely assistant in a box and cut her in half.

4 Pull a ~~tiger~~ ~~giraffe~~ lion crunchy, delicious taco out of a hat!!

Kayley read the list and scratched her head. She ate another cookie. "Aren't magicians supposed to pull a **rabbit** out of a hat?" Kayley asked.

She crunched another cookie.

Molly shrugged. "I guess so, but I don't have a rabbit at home. Plus, if I pull a taco out of my hat, I won't even have to pack a lunch on Friday."

"That's true," Kayley said. "But I don't think I want to get cut in half. What if you put me back together wrong? What if my feet point the wrong way? I won't be able to tie my shoes."

Molly shrugged her shoulders. "But you could be the fastest backward runner in the whole school!"

"I don't know about this, Molly." Kayley handed the list back to Molly. "Do you know how to do all those tricks?"

Molly shook her head. "That may be a small problem," she admitted. "So far, my only trick is dropping cards on the floor. I need to learn some **REAL** magic."

Kayley patted Molly on the back. "You need to learn the magic words," she said.

"Magic words?" Molly asked. "Do you know them?"

Kayley nodded. "Watch!" she said. **"Abracazoombadiddle."**

Kayley popped the last cookie in her mouth. She held out the empty cookie container. "I made all the cookies disappear!"

Chapter 3

Taco Hat

After school that afternoon, Molly walked into the living room. Mom was reading a book to Alex.

"Ladies and Gentlemen" Molly announced. "Well, Lady and Drooly Baby, I guess. Presenting . . . **Magic Molly**, the most amazing, magical magician in the entire universe."

Mom closed the book. Alex squealed and clapped his hands. **"Mol! Mol! Mol!"** he sang.

"Prepare to be amazed," Molly said. She held up her favorite blue baseball cap. It was wet and dripping.

"Molly?" Mom said.

"Don't ask," Molly told her.

"I'm asking," Mom said. "What is dripping from your hat?"

Molly held the hat in front of her. She waved her hand over it. **"Abrakadoodlediddle."**

She plunged her hand into the cap and pulled out a soggy handful of salsa, lettuce, and broken taco shells.

"TA-DAAAAAH!" she sang. "I pulled a taco out of my hat!"

Mom gasped and hopped to her feet. "Molly! The floor! What are you doing?"

"I'm doing magic!" Molly said.

Mom put Alex in his playpen and ran over to Molly. She cupped the hat in her hands.

"You're making a mess," Mom groaned. She quickly carried the dripping hat back into the kitchen.

Molly followed her. "I didn't expect that to be so messy," she admitted. "Or drippy."

Mom dropped the mess in the sink. She wiped her hands and gave Molly a towel. "Wipe your hands, please, Molly."

Molly wiped her hands. "It's a good thing I wasn't sawing Kayley in half that time. That probably would have made an even bigger mess. I might need a tarp for that trick."

Mom handed Molly some paper towels. "Please help me wipe up the floor," she said. "And tell me why you dumped salsa and lettuce and taco shells into your hat."

Molly wiped the floor. "I was getting ready to show the class an **amazing** magic trick for Show and Tell on Friday, because dropping cards on the floor is actually a pretty lame trick."

"So you thought that dropping salsa on the floor would be more amazing?" Mom asked.

"It was supposed to magically turn into a taco," Molly said. "I don't know what went wrong. I guess I said the magic words wrong. Kayley taught them to me at recess today."

"Molly," Mom sighed. "You can't just dump food into your hat and say magic words. Magicians have to learn how to do tricks. They have to practice."

"I don't have time to practice," Molly said. "Show and Tell is on Friday. I need to learn fast. How do magicians learn this stuff?"

"They probably read **books** about magic," Mom said.

"There are books that teach you how to do **real magic?**" Molly gasped.

"Of course," Mom said. "How did you think magicians learn tricks?"

Molly shrugged. "Magic school?"

"Maybe," Mom said. "But you should start with a book."

"I will!" Molly said. "And then I'm going to need a giant saw. And a tarp. Just in case."

"A saw and a tarp?" Mom asked.

"Don't ask," Molly told her.

Chapter 4

Super Librarian

The next day at the library, Mrs. Ross read the class a story about a boy who ran around the house wearing his underpants and a red cape. He thought he had superpowers. Then she asked the class a question. "If you could have any superpower, what would you choose?"

"I would be able to **fly!**" said Marianne. "And I would fly to Hawaii every day!"

"I would be able to turn **invisible**!" said Tori. "And I would escape from school and go to the beach! And then I would be invisible on the beach so I wouldn't get a sunburn!"

"I would have **laser eyes!**" said Ian. "I would blast holes in the wall and catch bad guys!"

Molly waved her hand in the air. "I would have the power to pull a **crunchy, delicious taco** out of a hat!" she cried. "And I could saw my lovely assistant in half and not make a mess on the floor!"

"Somehow I am not surprised about that," laughed Mrs. Ross.

The class got up to choose books.

Molly ran over to Mrs. Ross. "Mrs. Ross! Mrs. Ross! I need help!"

Mrs. Ross put her hands on her hips and puffed out her chest. "**Super Librarian** at your service, Molly. What can I do for you?"

Molly's eyes grew wide. "Are you **really** a superhero in disguise?" she gasped.

Mrs. Ross bent down and whispered in Molly's ear. "All librarians are superheroes in disguise," she said. "How can I help you?"

Molly smiled. "I want to be **VERY** Magic Molly by Friday. But I'm having some trouble with the magic part, so I'm just plain old Molly."

"I see," said Mrs. Ross.

"My magic isn't very good. So, instead of sawing my lovely assistant in half, all I can do is drop cards and make my hat all drippy, which isn't very magical at all," said Molly.

Mrs. Ross frowned. "I'm not sure that I'm following you, Molly."

Molly took a deep breath. "I saw Amazing Marvin do magic. I want to learn how to do **real** magic so I can be **Magic Molly**. Then I can show the class some amazing tricks on Friday."

"Ahhh!" Mrs. Ross said. "I've got it."

She led Molly across the library and pointed to some books. **"TAAA-DAAHHH!"** she sang.

"Will these books teach me how to do **real**
magic?" Molly asked.

Mrs. Ross nodded.

A huge smile spread across Molly's face.
"Wow," she said. "This is going to be great."

Chapter 5

Droopy Wands and Plastic Thumbs

Later that afternoon, Molly was hard at work in her room.

"**Knock knock!** Anybody home?" Dad said from the doorway. "Hi, Honey. How's it going?"

Molly held up a crumpled tube of paper. It was covered with dripping glue and glitter.

"Not so good," Molly said. "My wand is kind of droopy."

She pointed to the glitter. "And all the magic sparkles are dribbling out."

"Mom told me that you are trying to learn some magic tricks," Dad said.

"Yeah," Molly said. "I need to be able to saw my lovely assistant in half by Friday. And I also need to be able to put her back together again. She is probably going to be picky about that part. I got some magic books out of the library, but they were not full of magic."

"They weren't?" Dad asked.

Molly sighed. "No. I thought they would be full of **real** magic spells. But instead, they were full of tricks like making coins disappear. Why would I want to make money disappear?"

Dad laughed. "I guess you're right."

Molly patted Dad's arm. "I usually am," she said. "So instead of magic words, I thought I needed a **magic wand.**" She put her droopy wand on the desk. "But that's not working out well, either."

"Well," Dad said, "I have some good news. I found my old magic kit in the attic!" Dad held up a box with the words **"Dr. Amazmo's Super Deluxe Magic Kit"** on it.

"Wow!" Molly cried. "A **real**, official **Super Deluxe Magic Kit!**"

Dad opened the magic kit. "Let's see what we have in here," he said. He poked around in the box. There were lots of little pieces in it.

"Where are the magic words that I need to say to saw my assistant in half without making a mess on the floor?" Molly asked.

"I don't know if I can help you with a trick like that, Molly. You shouldn't be sawing anyone in half!" Dad said.

"Oh, I know you can't help me put Kayley back together," Molly said. "I saw you try to put the toaster back together that time you tried to fix it. I don't want Kayley to wind up in 50 zillion pieces like the toaster. Also, I don't think Mom would want me to say the magic words you were using when you fixed the toaster."

Dad reached into the box and took out a small, yellow scarf. He waved the scarf in the air. He twiddled his fingers and said, "Prepare to be **amazed.**"

He tucked the scarf into his hand and closed his fingers over it. He wiggled his fingers in the air over his closed hand. "And now, the magic words . . . **Presto-changeo, mumbo-jumbo, higgledy-piggledy!**"

He opened his hand and the yellow scarf was gone.

"WOW!" Molly said. "How did you do that?"

Dad smiled and waved his hands in the air. "It's **MAGIC!**" he said.

Molly pointed at his hand. "Um, excuse me, sir. What do you call that?"

A tiny piece of yellow scarf was poking out from the back of his thumb.

Dad smiled and blushed. "You caught me," he said. "I guess I should have practiced a little more."

He held out his hands and showed Molly a plastic thumb that he had slipped over his own thumb. The yellow scarf was tucked inside it.

"A fake, plastic thumb?"
Molly sighed. "That's not magic.
I want to do **real** magic. I want to
be like Amazing Marvin. Only
even better. I want to be **Magic Molly!**"

Dad smiled at Molly. "It takes years and
years of practice to be a magician like Amazing
Marvin," he said.

"I was kind of hoping to be a professional
by Friday," Molly said. "That's Show and Tell
day at school."

Dad stood up and patted Molly on the
head. He walked toward the door of Molly's
room. "I'm going to help Mom with dinner. You
can look through the magic kit and see what's
in there. I will be happy to help you learn a trick
or two if you want. But it takes time to get good
at anything. Lots and lots of time."

Molly poked through the box.

She found coins and cards and magic scarves. Then she found a long, shiny, black-and-white magic wand.

Molly smiled and waved the wand over her head. "I don't have lots and lots of time," she said. "But now I have this!"

Chapter 6

Coffee Magic

The next day at school, Kayley sat down next to Molly. "Hello, **Magic Molly!**" she said. "Have you been practicing for our big magic show on Friday?"

Molly smiled. "Nope," she said. "I don't need to practice anymore."

Kayley frowned. "I don't think that everybody is going to want to see you drop cards all over the floor for Show and Tell. I thought you wanted to do something **amazing.**"

Molly bounced her eyebrows. "Oh, I am going to do something amazing, all right," she said. **"Look at this!"**

She reached into her desk and pulled out the magic wand. "It's a **magic wand!**" Molly said. "It came from a **REAL** magic kit with a picture of a **REAL** magician on it. That means it has to do **REAL** magic!"

"Wow!" Kayley said. "How does it work?"

Molly waved the wand around a little. "I'm actually not sure about that. I can't find a power button on it."

"I don't think magic wands have power buttons," Kayley said. "I think you just have to point them and say the magic words."

Molly smiled. "My dad told me some magic words last night!"

"Not the ones he said when he fixed the toaster?" Kayley gasped.

"No! Real ones," Molly said.

"Try it! Try it!" Kayley sang.

Molly pointed the wand at Mr. Rose, who was sitting at his desk. She wiggled the wand and waved it gently in a circle. "**Pesto-Zesto, Tony-Baloney, Abracahooha!** Make Mr. Rose take a sip of his coffee!"

Mr. Rose reached over and took a long slurp from his coffee cup.

Kayley gasped.

"IT WORKED!" Molly cried.

"Molly Mac," said Mr. Rose, "it is quiet reading or writing time. What you are doing is the exact opposite of being quiet. Do I want to know why you are yelling in class?"

"Probably not," Molly said.

Molly quietly slipped the magic wand back into her desk and took out her sketchbook and a pencil.

"What are you doing, Molly?" Kayley whispered.

"My magic wand really works," Molly whispered back. "I'm making some big, big plans."

Chapter 7

Big Show at Big Rock

At recess, Molly raced across the playground, but she did not go to the secret snack spot. Kayley followed her.

"Molly! Molly!" Kayley yelled. "Our secret snack spot is over there! I brought more cookies that we can make disappear. Where are you going?"

Molly didn't answer her. She kept running until she got to Big Rock. It was a giant rock in the center of the playground. Molly climbed to the top of the Big Rock. Her magic wand was in her hand.

Kayley scrambled up Big Rock after her.

"Molly!" Kayley gasped. "What are you doing?"

Molly waved her magic wand in the air. "It works!" she said. "It really works. I can do **REAL** magic. I can make anything happen."

"I don't know," Kayley said. "I was thinking about that. Mr. Rose sips coffee all day. Do you really think you made him do that?"

"Oh, yes," Molly said. "This wand can do **REAL** magic. I will prove it!"

Molly waved the wand in the air and pointed it at some kids playing kickball. Lucinda rolled the ball toward Hameen.

"Hooky-Spooky, Cheesey-Weezey, Presteroni! Make Hameen miss the ball!" Molly said.

Hameen tried to kick the ball, but it rolled right past him.

"See?" Molly yelled. **"It works! It works!"**

Kayley shook her head again. "I don't know, Molly. Hameen is pretty bad at kickball."

Molly waved her wand in the air again. **"Attention! Attention! Ladies and Gentlemen!"**

Several kids stopped what they were doing and looked at Molly. **"Gather around! Gather around!"** she yelled. "Magic Molly is about to perform the most amazing magic trick in the entire world! She will be helped by her lovely assistant, Kaylala!"

Kids began to gather around Big Rock. Soon, there was a large crowd waiting to see Molly's amazing magic.

"I really think we should practice some more, Molly," Kayley said. "This is not a good idea."

"I know," Molly said. "It's a **GREAT** idea!"

Chapter 8

A New Plan

Swish! Swish! Swish!

Molly Mac waved her magic wand through the air. **"Attention, Ladies and Gentlemen!"** she announced. "Thank you for coming to Magic Molly's Amazing Magic Show! Prepare to be amazed as I saw my lovely assistant in half!"

Molly pointed to Kayley. The crowd gasped.

"Do you have the giant saw, Kaylala?" Molly asked.

Kayley shook her head. "Why would I have a giant saw in school? All I have is a plastic spoon for eating my apple sauce."

Molly frowned. "Since my lovely assistant didn't bring a giant saw to school, I will have to perform a different trick. Prepare to be amazed."

Molly waved her wand in the air. **"Pesto, Cheese-O, Baloney Maleezo!"** She pointed the wand at Kayley. "Float in the air, Kaylala!"

Kayley did not float through the air.

"That's not an amazing magic trick," said Carolyn.

"Let's go back to our kickball game," said Hameen.

The crowd started to walk away.

"Wait!" Molly yelled. "Wait! I have an even more amazing trick! **WAIT!**"

Molly hopped up and down.

SHOOOOOOP!

Molly's foot slipped. She scrambled and skidded across the rock. Then she toppled right off of Big Rock—rolling, twisting, and turning. Finally, she landed on her feet on the ground and tossed her arms up into the air.

Several kids cheered.

"Wow!" Kayley said. "That was amazing! You were like a circus acrobat!"

Molly looked down at her feet. "A circus
acrobat?" she asked. "Hmmm . . . Do you have
a flying trapeze and a giant net that I could
borrow for Show and Tell on Friday?"

"Do I even want to know why you want a
flying trapeze?" Kayley asked.

"Probably not," Molly told her.

All About Me!

A picture of me!

Name:
Marty Kelley

People in my family:
My lovely wife, Kerri
My amazing son, Alex
My terrific daughter, Tori

I really like: Pizza! And hiking in the woods. And being with my friends. And reading. And making music. And traveling with my family.

When I grow up I want to be:
A rock star drummer!

My special memory:
Sitting on the couch with my kids and reading a huge pile of books together.

Find more at my website: www.martykelley.com

MORE

MOLLY MAC

Meet Molly Mac, the curious
girl who is always onto
something. She's a whirlwind
full of questions, and she's
out to find the answers!

≥ Campground Creature ≤
by MARTY KELLEY

≥ Lucky Break ≤
by MARTY KELLEY

≥ The Best Friend Bandit ≤
by MARTY KELLEY

≥ Three...Two...One...Blastoff! ≤
by MARTY KELLEY

Sammy's Great Escape
by MARTY KELLEY

≥ Top Secret Author Visit ≤
by MARTY KELLEY

THE FUN
DOESN'T STOP HERE!

Discover more at
www.capstonekids.com

★ Videos & Contests
★ Games & Puzzles
★ Friends & Favorites
☆ Authors & Illustrators